Wende and Harry Devlin

PARENTS' MAGAZINE PRESS/NEW YORK

Copyright © 1978 by Wende and Harry Devlin
All rights reserved
Printed in the United States of America
10 9 8 7 6 5 4 3 2 1
Library of Congress Cataloging in Publication Data
Devlin, Wende.
    Cranberry mystery.
    SUMMARY: Maggie and Mr. Whiskers go in search of thieves who are stealing many valuable old things in Cranberryport.
    [1. Mystery and detective stories]   I. Devlin, Harry, joint author. II. Title.
PZ7.D49875Cr [E] 78-6219
ISBN 0-8193-0972-9   ISBN 0-8193-0973-7 lib. bdg.

For Christopher Devlin Gates

R ed leaves—yellow leaves—orange leaves! It was a beautiful Indian summer, but strange things were happening in Cranberryport—mysterious things.

At Grandmother's house on the edge of the cranberry bog, a great copper kettle disappeared. From the town hall a gold weather vane had been taken, and an old striped pole was missing from the barbershop.

Neighbors were beginning to eye one another uneasily.

"Could it be the new butter-and-egg man?" asked the grocer.

"It's always the old things that are taken. I wonder if it's that writer who lives in the red barn?" asked the butcher.

When a grandfather clock was stolen from the mayor's house, he hurried downtown and offered a $100 reward for its return. Almost in tears, he explained to the sheriff that the clock had been in his family for two hundred years. Maggie felt very sorry for him.

"I wish we could help," said Maggie to her sea-captain friend.

"Suffering codfish, I could sure use that reward," mused Mr. Whiskers. "I need a motor for my boat."

The sheriff scoffed when Maggie and Mr. Whiskers offered their services.

"Tend to your clamming, Mr. Whiskers. And as for you, Maggie, when a little girl catches a thief that I can't catch, I'll make her a deputy!"

A few days later, Mr. Whiskers lost a treasure himself.

After supper at Grandmother's and Maggie's house, he had trudged home over the sand dunes to his weathered cottage by the sea. As he opened the door, he was shocked to see overturned chairs, pushed-back rugs and ransacked closets.

Mr. Whiskers looked around the room. He caught his breath—Annabelle was gone! Annabelle, the carved figurehead from his grandfather's ship and his greatest treasure, was gone.

"Jumping sea cows, the blinkin' pirates are in for trouble now. No one is going to have my Annabelle," he said to himself in a fury.

Mr. Whiskers rushed out into the dusk and followed the drag marks in the sand to the ocean's edge. He looked out over the bay, but all he could hear was the lapping of water. All he could see was a small light in the purple darkness.

In the morning, when the sheriff learned of the new crime, he ordered his entire force into action. One man was sent to look for fingerprints. Another set up roadblocks. Deputies were assigned to cover auctions and antique stores to trace stolen pieces.

When Mr. Whiskers tried to sit down in the sheriff's office, the lawman was too busy to listen to the old sea captain's theory of where the robbers might be. So Mr. Whiskers wandered back to Grandmother's house. Casually, he suggested a picnic on Sailmaker's Island.

Grandmother wasn't interested. "How can anyone think about picnics when nothing is safe in Cranberryport," she sniffed.

But Maggie sensed that Mr. Whiskers had a reason. She asked Grandmother if she could pack a picnic basket. She promised to be home early.

Maggie, Mr. Whiskers and the picnic basket were soon off for the deserted island. Mr. Whiskers bent to the oars of his little boat. Maggie's brown hair streamed behind in the ocean breeze. "Someday, Maggie, I'm going to get a motor," puffed Mr. Whiskers.

The distance was short and the water calm. They were circling Sailmaker's Island when Maggie spied something ahead. "Look, Mr. Whiskers," she said in surprise, "there's a red boat tied in the cove."

"Aha!" chuckled Mr. Whiskers. He seemed delighted to find company on the island. "Let's have a look," he whispered.

Cautiously, they pulled the skiff up on the shore. Moving quietly, they searched the beach. Above the tideline, near some bushes, they discovered a pile of boxes, four fine old chairs, two desks and, to Mr. Whiskers' great excitement, a carved, wooden figurehead, half covered in an old sail.

Mr. Whiskers could hardly speak. "It's Annabelle!" he croaked. "Suffering codfish! The blinkin' pirates can't be far away!"

Silently, Mr. Whiskers and Maggie crept up to the abandoned sailmaker's shed. On tiptoes, they peeked into the windows and then, with great care, pushed open a side door. No one was in sight. The shed was filled with old mirrors, paintings and antiques, and the smell of wax and varnish filled the air.

"This must be where they fix up the old things," whispered Maggie. But the mayor's great clock was nowhere to be seen. "Maybe it's upstairs in the attic room," she said softly.

Maggie and Mr. Whiskers climbed the creaking stairs. Maggie had just discovered the mayor's clock in the attic room when they heard the door being slammed loudly behind them. Then they heard the rasp of a key turning in the lock. They were locked in.

Startled, Maggie screamed. Mr. Whiskers exploded. "Open up, you blinkin' pirates," he roared, banging on the door.

No one answered his shouts. There was only a mumble of rough voices downstairs.

A few moments later, Mr. Whiskers heard the sound of a motor and he rushed to the tiny window to look out. He saw one man in the red boat heading out to sea with his own little skiff tied behind and bobbing in the wake. Both boats were piled high with boxes and chairs.

"Maggie, we're marooned, stranded!" Mr. Whiskers threw his hat on the floor. "He's stolen our boat and picnic basket. We'll never get off this blinkin' island!"

They pressed their ears to the door and heard the sounds of the other thief in the small kitchen below.

Maggie began to think of Grandmother and how worried she'd be.

They had to get home!

While Mr. Whiskers stormed around the room, Maggie sat on a crate and thought. There were stout ropes on the boxes in the room. She knew she was small enough to get through the little window if Mr. Whiskers held the rope. And she could get back to the sheriff if she had something to float on.

"I have it!" said Maggie excitedly.

Despite Mr. Whiskers' worries and protests, Maggie was gently lowered out of the window. Mr. Whiskers sang "Sixteen Men On a Deadman's Chest" at the top of his voice so that the sounds of the knotted rope on the window would not be heard.

Maggie's mouth was dry and her heart beat wildly as she slowly swung down on the rope. What if the robber heard her?

She was relieved to feel her feet touch the ground, but still trembling, she made her way, from bush to bush, down the hill to where Annabelle, the wooden figurehead, lay. With great effort, Maggie dragged Annabelle on the old sail to the water's edge.

Taking one of the oars that Mr. Whiskers had stowed in the bushes, Maggie pushed the figurehead into the water and hauled herself aboard. Soon she was paddling Annabelle towards Cranberryport, grateful for an incoming tide and the last red rays of the setting sun.

From the attic, Mr. Whiskers' eyes never left Maggie until she was out of sight.

"Annabelle sails again," he said, "and Maggie must be the pluckiest captain she's ever had."

Annabelle Sails Again!

Now he turned to the work of loosening the hinges on the attic door.

Two hours later, he peered out the window that overlooked the bay. There was a full moon and the ocean was silver with light. He saw a boat moving into the waters of the cove. There were no lights on the boat and poor Mr. Whiskers could only hope it was the sheriff. "What if Maggie never made it," he groaned.

Mr. Whiskers' pulse quickened. Was it the thieves' or the sheriff's boat? He could wait no longer. From the far side of the room, he made a desperate lunge for the door. Mr. Whiskers burst through the panels with a thunderous crash! He hurtled down the stairs, bounced once and landed smack on top of a burly thief. Mr. Whiskers rose.

Groaning, the thief pulled himself up and ran for the door, into the arms of a tall man in a tan uniform.

The sheriff!

And right behind him stood two deputies and Maggie, in warm, borrowed clothes.

It was all over for the thief. He confessed that his partner would be back that night to collect the other stolen goods. One deputy marched him out to the boat and the sheriff ordered the other deputy to wait for the thief's partner to return.

"It looks as though you've turned up a real den of thieves," said the sheriff to Mr. Whiskers.

"I'm glad it wasn't anyone from Cranberryport," said Maggie.

The sheriff smiled as he turned to Maggie. "Here's the deputy badge I owe you. I want you to be handy whenever I have an important case. The reward is all yours, Maggie!"

"Oh, no," said Maggie. "Mr. Whiskers deserves it. He's the one who saw the lights on the island and suspected the thieves were here."

"We'll share it equally, Maggie," said Mr. Whiskers. "Let's buy a motor for my boat."

Much later, Grandmother hugged, scolded and welcomed Maggie and Mr. Whiskers into her kitchen. Dinner was roast chicken, sweet potatoes, cranberry pie and whipped cream.

Mr. Whiskers, who had been cross about missing his lunch, whooped, "Maggie, tonight I'm going to have two helpings of everything."

It was a great feast, but after all, who deserved it more than the pair who had solved the mystery of Cranberryport.

Grandmother's Famous Cranberry Pie-Pudding
(*Get Mother to help*)

6 tablespoons butter or margarine, softened
¾ cup sugar
1 egg
½ cup all-purpose flour
1 cup fresh cranberries, washed, stemmed, and dried
¼ cup chopped walnuts

Preheat oven to 350° (325° if using glass). Grease an 8-inch pie plate.

Cream butter and sugar until fluffy in a medium bowl; beat in egg, then beat in flour until blended. Stir in cranberries and walnuts. Spread evenly in pie plate.

Bake 45 minutes, or until firm and golden. Cool in pie plate on a wire rack. Cut into wedges. Serve warm or cold with whipped cream or vanilla ice cream.

Yield: 6 servings.

Recipe tested by the Food Department of Parents' *Magazine*